Vocal Science –
Flight to the Universe

Diana Yampolsky

© Copyright 2005 Diana Yampolsky.
All rights reserved. No part of this publication may be reproduced, stored in a retrieval system, or transmitted, in any form or by any means, electronic, mechanical, photocopying, recording, or otherwise, without the written prior permission of the author.

Note for Librarians: A cataloguing record for this book is available from Library and Archives Canada at www.collectionscanada.ca/amicus/index-e.html
ISBN 1-4120-7001-5

Printed in Victoria, BC, Canada. Printed on paper with minimum 30% recycled fibre. Trafford's print shop runs on "green energy" from solar, wind and other environmentally-friendly power sources.

TRAFFORD PUBLISHING

Offices in Canada, USA, Ireland and UK

This book was published *on-demand* in cooperation with Trafford Publishing. On-demand publishing is a unique process and service of making a book available for retail sale to the public taking advantage of on-demand manufacturing and Internet marketing. On-demand publishing includes promotions, retail sales, manufacturing, order fulfilment, accounting and collecting royalties on behalf of the author.

Book sales for North America and international:
Trafford Publishing, 6E–2333 Government St.,
Victoria, BC v8t 4p4 CANADA
phone 250 383 6864 (toll-free 1 888 232 4444)
fax 250 383 6804; email to orders@trafford.com

Book sales in Europe:
Trafford Publishing (UK) Limited, 9 Park End Street, 2nd Floor
Oxford, UK ox1 1hh UNITED KINGDOM
phone 44 (0)1865 722 113 (local rate 0845 230 9601)
facsimile 44 (0)1865 722 868; info.uk@trafford.com

Order online at:
trafford.com/05-1912

10 9 8 7 6 5 4 3 2

Diana Yampolsky

Yampolsky, Diana,

Vocal Science – Flight to the Universe

Copyright 2000

Published by:

Trafford Publishing

Edited by:

Alisa Yampolsky

and Steven Bottjer

Illustrations by:

Macksim Grunin

Toronto, Ontario, Canada

Cover Design by:

Macksim Grunin

Toronto, Ontario, Canada

Vocal Science - Flight to the Universe

4th Edition, May 2005

© Copyright 2000

All Rights Reserved.

If you are interested in personalized or group services regarding Vocal Science, please contact:

Diana Yampolsky

The Royans School for the Musical Performing Arts

Phone: (416) 229-0976

       1-888-229-TUNE (8863)

Fax: (416) 229-9184

www.vocalscience.com

www.vocalscience.com/totalcommunicator.html

www.vocalscience.com/royansuniverserecords

Acknowledgments

To my daughter Alisa, who I "grew up" with in the Canadian community, for her love and support and for helping to edit this book.

To Ted Kowalczyk, co-founder of the Royans School and who was with me from 1984-86 and forever. I am thankful for your direction and guidance always.

To Chris MacNeil for helping me to realize and bring out the great potential that was inside me.

To Steve Bottjer for writing assistance, understanding and friendship.

To my special friend Chris Wiker for his love and support.

To my past and present students for giving me the opportunity to perfect and apply the Vocal Science methodology.

To the innumerable friends and business associates who helped my business grow, including Mila Sak from MS Nova Consulting, Paul Sanderson & Associates, Betsy Powell from the Toronto Star, Betsy Vourantoni from Health with Herbs, Ann Rohmer from City TV, Mike Stafford at CFRB, Kim Geddes at TALK 640, Captain Frank from

Q107, Natasha Korolev of the Yonge Street Review, Kimberly Mason at Night Site, Riccardo Evangelista from Construction Word & Design, Robin Aube of Grant Avenue Studio, Courtney Betty of Betty & Associates, Brian Allen from Attic Records, Everett Ravenstein of Chalet Studios, Kim Cooke at Warner Music Canada, and too many others to mention.

To the many publications who have written about me or published my articles, including Canadian Musician, the Toronto Star and the National Post.

To the many broadcasters who have featured Vocal Science, including CITY TV's 'Breakfast Television', CFTO's 'EYE ON TORONTO', CP24 News, TALK 640, Q107, 103.5, CFRB, and many others.

To all the Engineers, Producers & Managers with whom I have worked to help my clients achieve their higher goals.

- Diana Yampolsky

About the Author

Diana Yampolsky is a Toronto-based Vocal Coach/Consultant and columnist for Canadian Musician magazine. Between spending 10 hours a day teaching at her school, The Royans School for the Musical Performing Arts, and helping singers achieve the best possible results in the recording studio, she also writes books and articles. She specializes in singing, performance and all aspects of total human development.

Diana takes pride in her present and former students' accomplishments, including: Raine of *Our Lady Peace* (Sony Records), Edwin (Sony Records), Brian Byrne of I Mother Earth (Universal Records), Lukas Rossi of Rise Electric, Nicole Hughes of *Scratching Post,* Monik Garo (A&M Records), Charlene Smith (Warner Music Canada), Diana Higgins of *Jane Doe,* Sabina Petermann (National Event Anthem Singer), David D'Amico of *Chronic Overboogie.* American clients include: Rob Mazurkiewicz (Singer, Songwriter, Producer), James Seney of *Sugarthorn,* Joe McCarthy of McCarthyizm (Lead Singer and Rhythm Guitar, David Julian of *Major Healy* (Backup Singer and Lead Guitarist) and many others…

Testimonials

Dawn Mandarino of the band Tuuli:
When I first picked up the Vocal Science: Flight to the Universe book, I couldn't put it down and finished it in one sitting. I was absolutely amazed that this book was contradicting everything I had ever been taught in the past about vocal performance. I wasn't even sure I could believe everything it said until I completed the vocal science course and discovered that all the techniques in the book actually worked! Everything from the facial muscle techniques to holding your stomach in actually made my voice feel stronger and allowed me to project my words more clearly. This book definitely provides a great starting point to anyone who wants to learn how to sing to their full extent. It's also quite funny and entertaining throughout!

**Dr.Patravoot Vatanasapt , Department of Otolaryngology,
Faculty of Medicine, Khon Kaen University, Khon Kaen, Thailand:**
"I would like to thank Diana for her wonderful book "Vocal Science- Flight to the Universe". The principle of her innovation is something different but comprehensible. Her book brought a holistic approach to vocal training and to a professional voice user. It's very helpful for my career in my voice clinic and also my sideline in music."

Captain Mark Reid, Regional Airline Pilot (Air Alliance):
"I had heard for a long time (over 10 years) of Diana's unique and exceptional teaching abilities... So - I was very excited to come across her book: 'Vocal Science - Flight To The Universe'. After reading it, I noticed an immediate improvement in my singing. I also discovered that I had developed, unknowingly, many bad habits over the years. Diana addresses these common bad habits in her very first chapter: 'How Not to Become a Singer (And Work Harder at Doing It)'! I would describe Diana as being the "Bruce Lee" of vocals: she has a non-traditional, yet suberb and perfect vocal technique that should be the standard throughout the world. Diana has helped me realize a long sought-after dream of being able to sing at a level that I once thought not possible! The book is worth every penny!"

Charlene Roy - "The Singing DJ", Chatham, Ontario:
"Vocal Science - Flight to the Universe is a must have book for singers and speakers of all levels of expertise. Diana explains in simple analogy the foundation that will allow you to reach your greatest potential as a singer. Diana's self-created Vocal Science destroys some of the popular myths on how to become a singer. Her examples make perfect sense and are easy to apply and the bottom line is amazing results! Diana delivers her knowledge with humor and examples that really sink in. Take it from a former student - Vocal Science works! Not only does it improve your singing, but also your self esteem and confidence. Vocal Science taps into a deeper level of a person's capability, sub conscience and inner creativity. Take care of your voice, invest in Vocal Science!"

Takeshi Okamoto - Singer/Songwriter, Tokyo, Japan:
"While I was in Japan I read Diana's postings on the Internet on her vocal techniques, which first inspired me to explore her method.
Her clear, straightforward explanations made it easy for me to try them out and hear and feel an immediate improvement in my singing. Because I felt that direct instruction would be necessary to fully appreciate her method, I decided to fly to Toronto to study with her. After only ten hours of training I have seen drastic improvement, and Diana has definitely made another believer out of me!"

Doug Smart of Eye Weekly & Lead Vocalist for the punk rock group One Down:
"After booking Diana's advertising for eye Weekly for over six months, curiosity recently got the best of me. I would read her ads and try to figure out exactly what Vocal Science was. As luck would have it, I managed to get my hands on a copy of Diana's book. After a thoroughly enjoyable read, I decided to take what I had learned in her book and apply it to my own singing. The results were immediately noticeable and Diana's techniques made singing not only easier, but far more enjoyable as well. I strongly recommend that all singers learn Diana's techniques immediately. Your voice will thank you for it."

Table of Contents

1. Introduction 11
   - Introducing Vocal Science 11
   - Discovery Stage 1976-1979 13
   - Research 1980-1989 15
   - The Birth of the Royans School for the Musical Performing Arts 16
   - Development Stage 1989-1994 22
   - Establishment 1994 – Present 26
2. How Not to Become a Singer (And Work Harder at Doing It!) 29
3. How to Become a Singer (And Work Smart Not Hard) ... 39
4. Vocal Science - Flight to the Universe 47
5. Assessing Your Instrument 55
6. The Physical Aspects of Singing 59
7. The Emotional Elements of Singing 63
8. The Intellectual Side of Singing 69
9. Vocal Impotence? In Need of Vocal Viagra? 73
   - A Few Words on Herbs 80
10. Vocal Science Magic – Curing the Tone Deaf and Rhythmically Challenged 83
11. The Total Performer - "Get a Life!" 89
12. Born Free - Vocally Yours Within the Structure 95
13. The Total Communicator – Speech to Singing 101
    - From a "Frog" to a "Prince" 103
    - Using Speech Exercises Towards Singing Excellence ... 108
14. More Music, More Business 113
    - Music and Today's Magic Technology 114
    - How Vocal Science Can Help 117
15. Who We Teach 119
16. Epilogue 125

Chapter 1: Introduction

I'd like to start this book by expressing my desire to "teach the world to sing". Even though I have been teaching all aspects of vocal development for almost 25 years, I would estimate that there are still "quite a few people" I have yet to reach! With this book we all have hope! I'm definitely planning to reach the entire Universe! And if the Universe doesn't come to us, we will simply have to take a flight to it! On this note, I would like to share with you my blueprints for how I am planning to do so.

Introducing Vocal Science

Vocal Science is a revolutionary vocal development technique for the new Millennium. The creation of Vocal Science started in 1976 when I, being a recent graduate of Leningrad's Music Teachers College, discovered something rather extraordinary. I sang and my throat did not hurt! Moreover, the sound was literally flying in perfect pitch and with perfectly clear projection! At this moment, I knew I was onto something.

Vocal Science - Flight to the Universe

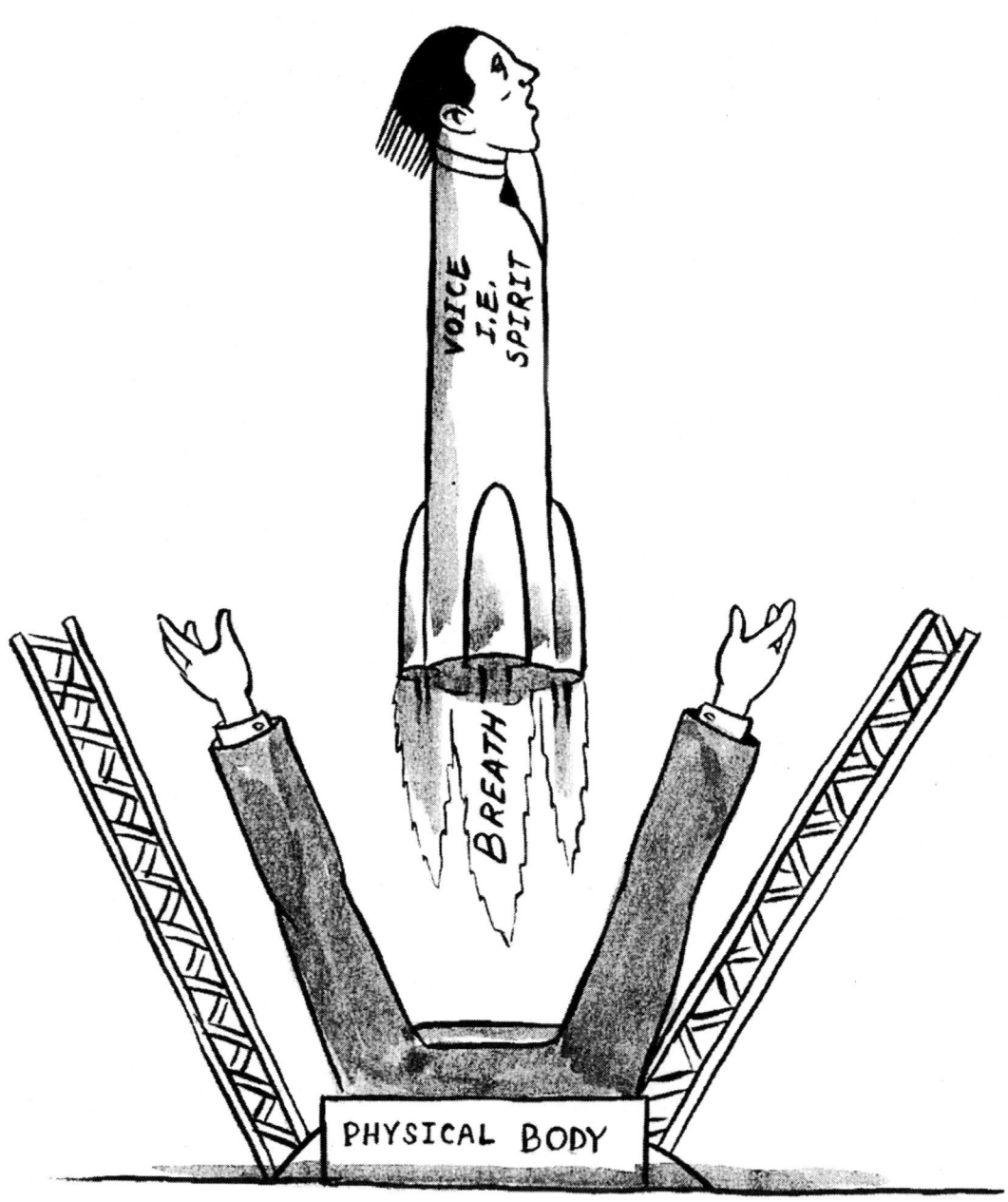

This is Neil. If Neil had taken off with the launching pad,
he would have never made it to the moon.

Discovery Stage 1976-1979

Entering Music Teachers College in 1972, after completing eight years of full-time music education in one of the most prestigious schools in Leningrad, I received pretty much the same vocal instruction as, I later realized, as did everybody else in the world. I was taught the traditional techniques such as dropping my jaw down and sticking my stomach out. Despite having difficulties specifically with such instruction, I still graduated at the top of my class, as all the other subjects at this institution were delivered perfectly. Therefore, up to this day, I'm thankful for the great overall music education I received and for the true love of music that was instilled in me. After graduation I got my first job working as a music teacher in a public school. My position consisted of primarily teaching students music and voice. With the former, my instruction was exemplary and very successful. But with the latter, I unfortunately still did not quite know what I was doing with regards to vocal technique.

As a singer myself, I was also getting the same sore throats and voice loss that most singers still complain about to this day. The truth is that I was well on my way to ruining my voice. Every day I was becoming more and more convinced that the traditional techniques that I had been taught didn't work. At this point I had no conscious idea of how to replace my traditional understanding of singing with something more beneficial.

Then one day a new song called *Yellow Leaves* was released and I performed it for my class. As I was singing I noticed a silence that was extremely unusual for a class of young kids. They appeared to be in awe of my performance. When I finished singing the children broke into ecstatic applause and told me they had never heard me sing in such an amazing way before. They were astonished by my voice and asked me why I sounded so great. My response was, "I don't know!" They begged me to sing the song again and I gladly complied. As I sang, I started to notice that my voice indeed sounded a thousand times better than it had before. Was this really me singing? It was like I was possessed! Furthermore, my voice didn't hurt – even on the high notes. My voice actually felt as different and as fantastic as it sounded. These performances had awoken something in my unconscious mind. It occurred to me that I had definitely discovered the basis for what could be a NEW vocal technique! However, I could not articulate or even fully understand what I had found. When I tried consciously to replicate my technique a third and fourth time I could not do it. In hindsight, I've come to realize that, while I had not consciously been trying to create an alternate vocal method, my subconscious mind had been working overtime to do so.

For a while my singing was going back and forth between new and old and good and bad. Sometimes I attained perfection in my vocals and other times, I did not. When singing beautifully, I was like a baseball player with a beautiful, natural swing -- I didn't question why it worked or understand the underlying mechanics, I just enjoyed it. But as time went on, I decided that I had to figure out what was happening in both instances and, more importantly, what I was doing right when I was singing exceptionally well. I came to the realization that the two modes of singing were in fact in almost complete opposition to each other and that when I did the opposite of what my teachers had told me to do, I could recreate the performance that had so amazed my students. I was intuitively projecting my voice upwards and off my vocal cords and it sounded clear and beautiful.

I realized that I was really onto something new and special and so I began to train my voice so that I lifted the sound off my vocal cords when I sang. Then I noticed that my abdominal muscles weren't working efficiently and so I sucked in my air instead of sticking my stomach out. This was the beginning of the second stage of Vocal Science: Research.

Research Stage 1980-89

Throughout the nine years that make up this stage, I developed the technique through experimentation and learned what worked and what didn't. I developed exercises that worked to improve a person's singing but did not yet completely understand exactly how they worked. During this stage, I started to compare singing to high-jumping. I was now aware that at its most basic, singing was all about taking off and lifting the voice off the vocal cords. I understood the basics enough that I knew I could help other singers, and at the same time fine-tune and expand my newly discovered technique.

I moved from Russia to Canada and started working as a private vocal coach. I applied everything I knew to my teaching, while at the same time translating my technique into English. Learning a new language was actually very important to my development because I also had to achieve an understanding of the syllables in the English language, as they were the key to proper singing. Today, almost twenty years later, I believe that my understanding of these syllables is definitely not any worse than that of the average Canadian.

The Birth of the Royans School for the Musical Performing Arts

In 1984, The Royans School for the Musical Performing Arts was launched by myself and my common law husband and partner, Ted Kowalczyk. Ted was a former opera singer who had become exposed to my new technique. We first met while singing in a choir together. From the first time he heard my voice, he was fascinated by its beauty and fullness and asked me if I would give him some lessons. I agreed and over the course of his instruction he was stunned by the results we achieved, which were by far greater than he had ever experienced in his previous years of education, (he was a graduate of the Warszawa Conservatory of Music). However, I still thought that the method was still rough at this point and, to be honest, I was still working mostly intuitively. That said, even though my method was far from what it is today, Ted's singing had been improved greatly. He became aware that he wasn't achieving his full potential as a singer and he later confessed that he realized that I could help him reach his peak when he first heard me sing and after experiencing my teaching firsthand. He also noted that I was the exact "opposite" of all the other voice teachers he had had in his life.

In Ted I found a kindred spirit. I had been training an "accomplished" opera singer who loved music and had been taught the same vocal techniques that my teachers had taught me. In time the love we shared for music grew into love for one another. Ted created the ideal conditions in which for me to develop my new technique and evolve as a vocal coach and performer. At this time, not only were we running a successful music school, but we also performed as a duo under the name Ted and Diana Royans. Our stage name Royans, created by Ted out of the blue, became our school name as well. Now, as I realize that I have gotten a little bit ahead of myself, I should also mention how the Royans School was actually born. While working at the Academy of

Music (owned by fellow Russian musicians), I met an older gentleman, 50 years my senior, who literally fell in love with my musical talent. He happened to be a polish immigrant, who during WWII ended up in Russia and, therefore, spoke Russian fluently. One day, I came to work early and sat down at the piano located in the front lobby of the Academy. At that time, I knew all the current Russian songs and romances and, while waiting for a student, I started to play and sing. Suddenly, I was interrupted by a male voice behind my back with the question, "Who are you?" I replied that I worked there as a singing and piano teacher and the person behind the voice seemed to be pleased but not quite satisfied with my answer. This puzzled me and this is how our conversation began. The gentleman stated that both my singing and playing were extraordinary and asked me why I had not opened up a school of my own. I laughed and informed him that I was a poor immigrant with a young child and did not have the sufficient funds to dare dream about it. Then he said that his life-long dream was to find somebody talented, young, vibrant and ambitious to operate a music school that he would fund. According to him, his late wife and relatives never took seriously his musicianship, nor his idea to open up a music school of his own. In reality, his piano playing was truly amazing, especially given his age. We continued our conversation and I started to realize that he was hinting that I would be the perfect candidate to run the music school of his dreams. At first, I thought this was some kind of joke but he definitely seemed to be very interested.

He was persistent and even found my home phone number through my current employers, whom he apparently knew. I have to admit I was a little bit scared and so I transferred all his phone calls to Ted. The elder gentlemen and Ted, both being polish, understood and connected with one another right away. Then I learned that Ted had taken a trip to Lake Simcoe to visit our new friend and our future sponsor. Ted returned in a shocked state bringing home with him quite a few musical instruments, which definitely had market value. According to Ted, this man didn't have anything else in his home except musical instruments and a whole bunch of pets *and* wild animals, which he fed night and day. Shortly after Ted's visit, this eccentric sweetheart continued to pursue us until he convinced Ted to drive to Lake Simcoe to pick him up and bring him to our place. Needless to say, we did not have any proper furniture or animals and except for the piano I brought all the way from Russia, no other musical instruments. Once again, he asked me to sing and play for him and as I finished he asked us to drive him towards the Royal Bank Building in downtown Toronto. When we arrived he left us in the lobby of the bank and disappeared with a bank representative. Approximately fifteen minutes later, he returned and handed me a certified cheque in the amount of eight thousand dollars with my name on it. He explained that we now had no choice but to open a music school – and the sooner the better! Ted and I looked at each other and admitted out loud that we now had no reason not to and felt very excited but scared…as neither of us knew anything about running a business!

So we opened the doors February the 15th, 1984 and had already used all the money our sponsor had given us. We were broke, but full of enthusiasm. Now we had to figure out how to find all the students we needed to pay our second month's rent as the first and last had been covered with our startup funds. Luckily for us, immigration in Toronto was in full swing and those coming from European countries were really anxious to educate their children. And since we were located in the heart of Little Italy, right beside two schools where I had previously worked as a singing and piano teacher, we enrolled 115 students in no time. We were very happy with this development; however, we had no clue about the "business" side of our venture. We had to learn about it the hard way – by hands-on experience. Music was all we really knew, but what we didn't know was how to put equal emphasis on the *Business* part of the equation. However here I must mention that the word *Music* was much bigger than it is nowadays and that is what helped us to survive! During the last fourteen years of running this business *by myself,* as unfortunately my best friend, partner and common-law husband Ted Kowalczyk passed away unexpectedly in 1986, I believe that I have gotten the *business* part down to a science. However, I do greatly regret that the MUSIC, which sustained my business from its birth, has diminished in its meaning. I know for a fact that if I were starting out today, the music by itself would be a very small vehicle to success and that makes me very sad. (Chapter 12, "More Music, More Business", discusses my beliefs about how music and business should be equal halves of the same whole.)

Looking back, between Ted's death in June of '86, through February of '87, when our first lease was about to expire and the building which housed our first location was sold to new owners, I was very emotionally drained and had to decide if I wanted to continue the school by myself or give up on it altogether, as I also had a six-year old child to take care of. Here I have to acknowledge two people who became very dear to me. Both were current students of the school and friends of the family: Marc Theberge and James Knapp. Both were Canadian actors that were studying voice at our school and also helped out with the school's many musical productions and events. They were a great moral support for me during this hard time in my life. Both volunteered their help at the school, especially in the administrative department about which I had no clue. In my weak moments when I contemplated giving up on the whole business idea, they were the ones persuading me that I COULD DO IT and assuring me that Ted would never forgive me if I did otherwise. I am still in communication with both Marc and Jim and will cherish their help and friendship FOREVER! Thank you Guys! I owe you BIG TIME!

By February 1987, I was running the school by myself and had to make a new decision because the new owners of my building wanted to drastically increase my rent: I had to either pay almost double or move on. Again, a student helped me greatly! I made the decision to move and found a new location with very reasonable rent, but needed approximately $10, 000 to renovate the space to the point where it would be suitable for the operation of the music school. This student's mother worked as a manager at a CIBC bank and, without any collateral or security offered by me, broke all the rules and loaned me $10, 000! Now the future of the Royans School was looking more prosperous. In March of 1987, I moved into my new location and decided to downsize the school. Now we were primarily specializing in vocal and piano instruction. We no longer had a retail music store or rehearsal space for bands, as neither the space nor my own capacity would permit their operation.

Shortly thereafter I realized that the one and only subject I was truly interested in specializing and offering to my clients was singing. Vocal Development became our specialty and, with this decision, things really started taking off.

Development Stage 1989-94

My confidence in the Vocal Science method was soaring as my students were saying great things about my teaching. People were literally "dropping their jaws" in amazement at how good they sounded. I, of course, had to remind them not to drop their jaw!

Another confidence builder was the fact that the school was still soaring even when the Province was in a deep recession. People knew that what I was teaching was special and were willing to pay for it even in tough times.

Until this point, I was still teaching and singing intuitively. In late 1989 I met Chris MacNeil, my future associate and husband, who was also central to my development. He was an accomplished musician and a brilliant human being. Our connection was infinite. With his help, my method, which had always been there
subconsciously in an abstract shape, became tangible. What Chris did was help me to properly spell it out in English and bring it out on a conscious level.

One important aspect of Chris's contribution was that he challenged me to be able to produce singers in just 10 hours! He also challenged me to offer an introductory session with guaranteed videotaped results! These ideas were very scary yet very exciting. The rationale was to present my school as offering something that was immediately apparent and different. The side benefits are that I am now able to reach more students and my clientele is more satisfied because they are spending less money and getting much quicker results. I have to admit that meeting these two challenges was probably equivalent to climbing Mount Everest, but after almost giving up on these ideas several times, I finally SUCCEEDED!

Vocal Science - Flight to the Universe

The stress of balancing the business, my personal life and my role as a mother to a still young child, was building up and wearing me down. One day I woke up and discovered that I had lost my voice. As you can imagine, this is paralyzing for someone in my position. After a few days of rest, I still could not speak, much less sing or teach. I could not understand what had happened because there was no warning – I had not been experiencing any pain or discomfort with my voice. I went to see several doctors and none could restore my voice or even tell me what was wrong. In the end, the loss of my voice was a blessing in disguise. I discovered what I consider to be an important part of the development of Vocal Science – that your voice reflects the state of your being, i.e. your mental, physical and emotional makeup. Further confirmation of this belief was given to me by a natural practitioner, herbalist and iridologist, Betsy Vourantoni, who since then has also become a dear friend and associate. I had been referred to her by a local Herbal Company, which had identified her as the best practitioner in the Province. After our first meeting, this was confirmed. After a thorough examination of my iris (using the science of iridology), her first words to me were that the loss of my voice had absolutely nothing to do WITH MY VOICE! I was shocked and relieved at the same time, but still found it hard to comprehend what she was telling me. According to Betsy, my thyroid gland (located in the middle of the throat) was shot, due to stress and suppressed emotions and hurts. (I should mention that the marriage between two musicians was, in spite of all the things we had in common, extremely rocky.) Now Betsy had to work on me holistically, balancing me emotionally on one hand and supporting my physical body, (building up my immune system), on the other. Within less than 24 hours of first seeing her, I had already experienced positive results and was sure I was *finally* on the right track to recovery. The cause was identified – the cure was obvious. Now, once again, I was entering a new phase. Gradually, I regained my voice, building it step by step, like a stroke patient learning to walk and speak again. It was not easy, but in the process I discovered a lot of interesting things about which I had no prior knowledge. Experientially, I learned that the more breath (support) I had underneath of my sound, the easier the note could be attacked and delivered to its aimed destination. Now I knew that not only would I recover my voice, but I also once again intuitively knew that I was on to something…

And surely enough, one night in 1994, I had a dream that described and explained in detail, each and every stage of the instruction that I had already been promoting to my students experientially, and that I knew worked. But what I had not known, was WHY it had been working !

As I later found out, this was not that unusual. Often the unconscious mind expresses itself in dreams. When I woke up, I knew exactly WHY everything I had been doing during my teaching sessions HAD

WORKED WITH ABSOLUTE EXCELLENCE! I could now justify every syllable, word, and note. I knew why the exercises I had created were beneficial, how speech was related to singing, and how singing related to the soul. Both Research and Development stages were now complete.

Establishment 1994 – Present

I am now in what I call the Establishment stage. This consists of teaching Vocal Science to as many people as possible through private lessons and seminars. An important part of this stage is to also train other teachers to be able to coach others using this method. (Afterall, I definitely want Vocal Science to live on and benefit people even when I am no longer around and in, hopefully, a better place.) Therefore, in essence, this stage is about making Vocal Science an established technique among musicians, music educators and music lovers. My goal is to expand my business worldwide and present as many people as possible with the opportunity to benefit from Vocal Science.

The following stage is, in my mind, called Completion. Does it mean that this is it? How will I know? Will I have another dream? Or will I just get older? I think none of the above. I will only know that my mission has been completed when the Vocal Science method is recognized worldwide as the ONE AND ONLY!

Entering a new millennium and evaluating the previous one in which most of my life has taken place, I can only speculate that our lives will be moving at an even faster pace and, hopefully, more efficiently, and therefore, more productively. The Vocal Science method is definitely compatible with all the demands of the new century.

Chapter 2: How Not to Become a Singer (And Work Harder at Doing It!)

I thought that in this chapter I would vent a little of my frustration and also have some fun while sharing some of the insights I've gained over the years regarding myths about learning how to sing.

Since everyone knows it takes years of arduous work to become even a moderately good singer (myth #1), for once I'll go with the status quo and add what I know to it, so as to assist people in working harder at taking even longer at it. Most people have this under control, so this chapter is to keep it that way and is also for those few who may be breaking this long tradition (like myself) and doing it faster, easier and more naturally.

The first point is to be sure and *drop your jaw while singing* (a little is good but more is better) because it traps the sound in the throat preventing it from being lifted off the larynx to the upper palate, through the four main vocal chambers or cavities and outward with anything close to your maximum power.

The second, and equally important point, is to *sing from your diaphragm and push your stomach out.* This prevents the upper diaphragm from expanding fully, therefore limiting your air supply and increasing the likelihood that you'll run out of air depending on the length of the note or phrase you're singing. An excellent way to train yourself for this is to lie on the floor and find yourself a nice thick book to place on your abdomen (the Toronto phone book works great) and "pump paper" up and down until you can stick that stomach out so that even a punch won't phase you. Then you'll be sure that the upper diaphragm will never open fully.

"This is Fred. He's mastered the technique of dropping his jaw. Doesn't he look great?"

Next, you should *sing with your speaking voice,* i.e. sing each syllable of your lyrics using your vocal cords with your chin down and without any support or structure to it, ("closing" each syllable), which characteristically produces a "pear" shaped opening inside the mouth and cuts the sound short, making it less than truly singable. This will help avoid lifting the sound off of the vocal cords, bouncing the sound off the upper palate, ("opening" the syllable), and projecting the properly structured sound outward, which produces a round "apple" shaped sound inside the mouth and making the sound, *unfortunately, more singable.* (This is also, by the way, why people with accents tend to lose them while singing.)

While we're on the subject of the shape of things, be sure and *breathe only through the nose* because it tends to make the shape inside the mouth more elongated or banana shaped and the sound more nasal. *Great, eh?*

*"This is Frank. He's working really hard!
Too bad this won't give him abs of steel!"*

Another way to make more work for yourself, (and have less as a singer), is to make certain that as far as your head goes, you sing only with your jaw and mouth, including your tongue and lips. This excludes the use of your facial muscles and reduces the likelihood that any resonance in those nasty head cavities I mentioned earlier will take place, causing your sound to be amplified, *(God forbid)*, and unavoidably reflected off the upper palate and projected outward to the audience.

Tilting the head back is very important since it directs the trajectory of the sound away from the audience. This is particularly useful in bands because it not only means that you will have to put more energy into getting the sound out to the audience but it also means that you will be directing some of the sound back behind you to set a proper example for any of your band members that might be developing a "natural" singing voice.

"This is Mike. Only the walls can appreciate his singing! Too bad the audience is not getting their money's worth!

Bending your knees is a great technique for limiting your power as a singer. Since sound is a physical thing, bending your knees changes the ratios relating to your height and the arc of the trajectory for the sound will cover much less distance, *which is what you want right?*

Another very relevant issue that I will cover in detail in later chapters, and that I'll just touch on here, is diet. One of the single most important causes of throat problems with singing is mucous. Sound can't lift off of thin air - it lifts off the vocal cords. Dancers don't dance on carpet, they dance on hardwood floors. This is so they can get a proper lift. *In the same way, you can prevent a really sharp "lift" with each and every note you're singing if you have lots of mucous and phlegm on your cords and in your system.* The best foods to eat to get this way are animal products especially beef, pork, milk, eggs and cheese, (although *all dairy products will do a really great job of getting you there).* Foods to avoid would be mucous burning foods and herbs, (cayenne tops the list), or fresh fruits and vegetables, grains, legumes and anything else whole and unprocessed that doesn't have a face.

One of the best ways to practice not becoming a singer, which I personally know of, is to sing scales. If you look even superficially at the songs you're singing, you'll see that they are composed of a finite number of specific combinations of sounds, duration's and pitch.

"This is George. Even a crane can't straighten his knees and lift his sound upward!"

Singing scales has nothing whatsoever to do with developing your ability to anticipate them in any song. So, *sing lots of scales and don't worry,* no one either in Russia, (my teachers were the best available), or here in the West, has EVER made any connection between scales and training the voice to sing properly! So there's no danger of you becoming a quickly accomplished singer with this approach.

Finally, *be sure and spend time working on each of these exercises individually and never collectively* because even the thought of integrating or harmonizing the various aspects of your singing might slow you down in your efforts to hinder your singing progress *and that would never do.*

So work long and hard, and whatever you do, if you want to avoid rapid easy vocal development at any level, then DO NOT READ the following chapters in this book and stay as far away as you can from the ROYANS SCHOOL and ME.

Chapter 3 - How to Become a Singer (And Work Smart Not Hard)

In the previous chapter, entitled "*How Not to Become a Singer (And Work Harder at Doing It)*", I humourously outlined some of the common pitfalls that befall many aspiring singers. In this chapter, I would like to present you with a sequel of sorts and provide you with some proactive information on how you might QUICKLY and EFFICIENTLY improve your singing.

The first, and most important thing, is to understand that it is a complete myth that it takes years of hard and arduous work to become even a moderately good singer. I have created an accelerated vocal instruction method called Vocal Science, which allows a beginner to become a professional singer within just 10 hours. (In fact, at my school, the Royans School for the Musical Performing Arts, IT IS GUARANTEED!) Here, it is important to define what I consider a 'beginner' to be. A beginner is a student who has adequate musical ability and a high level of determination and intelligence. In essence, a 'beginner' is only missing the *technical* knowledge of singing. Throughout my experience, the majority of beginner students are already in bands and are performing at least semi-regularly. I consider all other students to be 'pre-beginners' and it usually takes about 20-30 hours of instruction to transform them into a semi-professional or professional sounding singer. In both instances, development occurs very fast and most definitely does not take years. Now that we have dispelled this myth, let's look specifically at how we can dispel many others.

The myth of dropping your jaw while singing, which I mentioned in 'How Not to Become a Singer', is especially damaging to the progress of any aspiring singer. (I have actually had students who have told me they have literally been trained to do this.) Once you drop your jaw down, the sound falls down to your throat, splits your vocal cords, falls between them and then goes to your stomach and dies at your feet. (This is what I call 'Vocal Impotence' - it's flat, it's down and it's not performing upon command.) Now you should take action! Firstly, let me explain that the sound begins between your upper and lower teeth and travels above your breath, which becomes the driving force for your voice. If you put your arms up, around and above your head, you will see that your head is inside of a perfect circle. If you drop your jaw down, the entire sound falls down along with it and the circle is now approximately 390 degrees, which according to the laws of physics and geometry cannot exist. This means that the correct height for the proper flight of the sound cannot be accomplished. At this point, your sound is flying dangerously low and will inevitably crash. Therefore, I believe that if you lift your cheekbones high enough, (and leave your lower jaw completely alone), in conjunction with the proper support of your lower abdomen and upper diaphragm, your sound will achieve a smooth, safe and pleasant flight to its aimed destination.

"This is John. The way he lifts his sound off of his vocal cords in trying to sing is equivalent to a plane taking off with the airport in trying to fly. In both instances, their altitude is dangerously low, and a crash is therefore inevitable"

Another myth that I would like to dispel is that which says you should *push your stomach out while singing*. Given that the breathing mechanism consists of 3 components: the lower abdomen, which is responsible for the height of your sound; the upper diaphragm, which is responsible for the width of your sound; and the mouth/breath, which flies underneath of your sound to propel the sound forward, when you stick your stomach out you are actually preventing the entire breathing mechanism from working correctly.

To use an analogy that everyone is familiar with, I will refer to several scenes from the movie *Titanic*. At the beginning of the movie, there were several scenes that showed the engines at the bottom of the boat and gave some idea of how it worked. Apparently, these scenes made some people feel slightly impatient, as they were more interested in the upcoming love story than anything else. However, as the story progressed, it became clear why these scenes had been so carefully drawn out. Just after the boat had hit the Iceberg, they showed the engines again, only now they were no longer producing the required pressure to keep the ship afloat. Subsequently, a passenger asked the man who designed the *Titanic* how long it could stay afloat. The engineer who previously claimed that the boat was unsinkable now knew definitively how long it would take for the entire ship to sink.

The same principles apply to your voice when there is no air and support underneath of the sound. Curiously, I have always wondered why the majority of students are taught to stick their stomach out when all fitness professionals will tell you to hold your stomach in while doing an exercise that requires oxygen. In order to prevent your voice from drowning, you must *tuck your stomach in,* open up your upper diaphragm as much as the length of the phrase being sung requires, take the mouth breath and shoot your sound on top of your physical body and your 'Titanic' will definitely prove itself unsinkable!

Another myth that needs to be dispelled is that which claims that you should tilt your head backwards while singing. (Needless to say, this is equivalent to the Titanic sailing back to the port from which it left rather than towards its destination.) In other words, the direction of the sound will be completely erroneous because it is not being directed towards the audience and thusly would take that much more effort to accomplish the delivery of your performance. A related myth that I would like to contradict is the one that says you should bend your knees while singing. If you follow this notion, your sound will be flying low and again threatening to crash. Because the arc of the sound will be low, the trajectory will be that much shorter than if the singer had applied the whole mass of his body to catch the necessary momentum to establish the proper height and depth in the arc to allow the inertia to complete the destined flight.

"This is Grace. She's trying to dance while sticking her stomach out. Not so graceful, is she?"

Finally, I would like to point out the futility of singing scales as a form of practice. In all my experience, I could never comprehend the benefit of applying these scales into actual singing. The common notion that they warm up your voice is completely obsolete. Nobody was ever able to make an actual connection between these useless exercises and actually singing a song properly. For example, in ballet, the dance consists of certain movements as well as five positions of the arms and feet. Ultimately, any ballet dance will consist of these components, which were practiced separately and in conjunction with each other much before the dance was born. Now the dancer is ready to put on the costume and connect all these parts and movements simultaneously, thus creating an artistic form out of previously separate components. Similarly, it is of utmost importance that all parts of the singing mechanism work together but these parts should be first practiced separately and only then put together for the wholesome performance.

To conclude this chapter, I would suggest to all of you to adopt the motto "work smart, not hard", - small effort for maximum results!

"This is Belle. She is doing her bar exercises to perfect and precode her movements."

Chapter 4: Vocal Science - Flight to the Universe

In this chapter, I would like to seriously offer a different approach that will hopefully help you learn how to reach your full potential as a singer. Whenever I conduct one of my educational seminars, I always start by saying to the audience that I did not come here to prove anybody wrong or to prove myself right; I came to offer something different and you can accept it or reject it. And on that note, I would like to talk about two things that may at first seem different or even rather conflicting in nature: Science and Spirituality. Your first response may be something along the lines of "I hated science in high school" or "I sing rock music not gospel." Therefore, I would like to invite you to open your mind and entertain the possibility of seeing yourself and your voice in a completely different way.

I call my method of vocal instruction Vocal Science because I believe that I have developed a proven scientific method of producing sound, as well as the best possible vocal performance. The first point to recognize is that sound is a physical material body and it travels as such upon the laws of physics and geometry. The second point is that you can compare your body to a very complex, high-level computer, where your anatomy and physiology represent the hardware. As you probably know, software is an algorithm, essentially a set of instructions, and hardware is useless unless you have the proper software running on it. Your brain is like a computer's CPU and everything you do, (i.e. walking, talking, eating), is essentially the process of running software. The act of singing works the same way, and your voice is the output resulting from your physical hardware and your software, i.e. training or lack thereof. Unfortunately, we cannot simply drive to Radio Shack and buy the software that will make us a great singer (or painter, or athlete or doctor). WE acquire our software through learning. There are two ways you can learn: through your own experience or by having someone teach you. When I start instructing students, I not only have to give them the proper program, but I have to DEBUG or UNINSTALL the previous software or deal with a "VIRUS" on their system that they have somehow caught. Then through the method of visualization and special exercises we can access the cell in the speech center of your brain, (Broca's Area), which is responsible for the voice, (singing and speaking), and input the instructions that will allow it to do exactly what we want it to.

In almost a quarter century of teaching, I have discovered that there are four components that make up the mechanism which allows your voice to reach its fullest capacity: Physical Support of your body, structure, placement of the sound and, as a final outcome, the projection of the sound to its aimed destination. Complying with these components will guarantee that there is no pain or strain on your vocal anatomy.

"This is Bill. He finally obtained Vocal Science software. Now as Bill's system is 'virus-free', a successful performance is assured"

There is one thing that sets human beings apart from complex machines running algorithms: our spirits. In many ways, singing is a lot like the martial arts. Most Martial Arts are not only techniques for fighting or self-defense, but are also philosophies of how to live your life. They consist of good technique and a spiritual component.

I approach singing in the same way. Good technique is the basis upon which a singer's spirit is free to soar. It is your spirit (along with your completely individual physical body, i.e. no two people have the exact same DNA) that makes you different from anyone else and makes you unique. (Why try to sound like Celine Dion or Mick Jagger. The world already has one of each.) Only when you sing with proper technique are you able to project a voice that is purely yours and reflects your INDIVIDUAL self. It is your spirit that separates a technically good performance from one that is truly authentic. Many of my past and present students have not only developed good technique but have improved in all aspects of their life or have changed their lifestyle completely. They are healthier, more positive, and more fulfilled.

Diana Yampolsky

"This is Annie. She's lost her balance because her technique was faulty!"

The process of learning proper balance for singing will result in more balance in your life. Conversely, a singer with incorrect technique cannot give a truly special performance because their spirit, (voice), is inhibited by "bugs" or "viruses" in their software. Many people come to me, dying to express their emotions through their voice. I help them to discover and uncover it and let it soar. The congruency of the physical sound and the emotional rapport with the audience produces the desired total performance, i.e. combination of technical skill and artistic merit.

Vocal Science is at its most basic an alignment of the subconscious mind, conscious mind, and the physical body, which are then put into total integration and synergy with each other. This is the formula for the ideal vocal performance. By using specially designed exercises with the appropriate repetition, you can program your mind so that when you sing, you will perform many of the technical aspects of singing subconsciously. Seventy-five per cent of your performance will come out on automatic pilot and you will need only a small amount of conscious effort to put your performance in place. Your physical body is the condition of your hardware; your spirit is the individual intangible that will make your voice and performance something that is unique and reflective of your state of being.

The release of your spirit into the performance of a song is dependent upon using the correct technique.

Diana Yampolsky

"This is Bruce. He is so focused that he can sing AND throw a punch at the same time without even breaking a sweat!"

The act of singing is then a combination of good technique and individual identity. I have titled this book to reflect my belief that a scientific approach to vocal instruction is what will allow your voice (i.e. spirit) to take flight and soar. I will expand upon these ideas and provide more detailed information in the following chapters.

Chapter 5: Assessing Your Instrument

I would like, in this chapter, to talk about the fascinating aspect of singing which concerns the ratios or proportions of the various parts of your instrument, i.e., your physical body. I have found that there is a direct link between a person's natural singing ability and the proportional size of the various body parts as they compare to one another. This is a very useful distinction not only in teaching, but for anyone who is interested in knowing where they stand in terms of natural ability.

What specifically, do we mean when we're talking about your "instrument"? You can divide the body into two main divisions - upper and lower. The upper body consists of your upper abdomen and back, chest, lungs, throat, vocal cords, facial muscles and head cavities. The lower body is made up of your lower abdomen and back, buttocks and legs. The hip area divides them, (you could draw a line across the middle of your abdomen.)

At this point, I have to interject with a small reminder. As singers, more than anyone, you must make the distinction between you and your instrument. It's painfully apparent that most people take it for granted, and don't look at there body like a musician looks at their instrument. No self-respecting musician would ever consider exposing his guitar or drums to corrosive chemicals or other types of toxic materials, yet what else do we do to our so-called "instruments" when we singers eat junk food or (God forbid!) "road" food?

The components listed above make up your instrument. What's most important, initially, is not to consider how well or poorly you can use these parts, but rather, their proportion to one another. You see, the size of every component in the system affects the quality of its output. A shorter person usually has thin, short vocal cords, which allow higher notes to be sung but limit the amount of "body" or fullness in their sound. Generally speaking, a larger person has more "body" to resonate the sound off of, which produces a fuller sound.

Here's an analogy. A violin makes music because the sound created by the vibrating strings resonates off its "body". Depending on the gauge and age of the strings, the thickness and quality of the wood, and its weight, that sound is pleasing in varying degrees (assuming that the actual skill of the player is the same in all cases). With the body, it's the same. Each part has a significant effect on the musical output that the instrument will produce. In the case of your body's parts, the pertinent issues are height, weight, width, depth, length and thickness.

Now, you can look at yourself and rate the proportional symmetry of your body. Using the middle of your abdomen as the centerline, is your upper and lower body equal in length, weight, etc.? I have found that the ideal body configuration for singing is between 5'8" and 6'2" weighing 170-200 lbs. for a man; and between 5'5" and 5'7" and weighing 130-140 lbs. for a woman with all cases being physically fit, meaning a well-toned body. A toned body is one that, for example, you can't "pinch an inch" of fat on. (This isn't to suggest that if you do not exactly match these proportions you cannot be an accomplished singer. It just means you will have work with what you have and make the most out of it.)

Now we can start to look a little deeper at the effects of proportion. Given that there is some disproportion in most people, it would be better (from a vocal standpoint) to have long legs and a shorter body than short legs and a longer body. In order to understand why this is so, we have to touch on some of the laws of physical mechanics that I employ in my vocal method.

If you want to throw a ball, how do you wind up for the pitch? Do you make a tight small circle or is it an arc that utilizes the full range of motion that your appendages will allow? What is the resulting trajectory or "flight path" of the ball? Does it shoot in a straight line out from your body like a shot put, or does it curve above your head and project upward and outward in a high-flying arc? Sound is just as physical as that ball, and must be handled accordingly. To be able to generate the trajectory for the sound that will reach the back of the room, you must be able to do so with the widest possible arc. Considering the part that the upper and lower diaphragm play in singing, which person can develop the widest arc when they are lifting and projecting that sound: the one whose mid-point is below the abdomen or the one with the mid-point above the abdomen? (Hint: imagine that instead of winding up to belt out a note, you're throwing that ball again. The lower center of gravity has it because of the greater arc of the trajectory.)

All parts, then, are important. No two singers are the same, and must be treated differently even though the desired outcome is the same. If you drive your eight-cylinder car as if you're in my four cylinder, you're going to run out of gas!!!

When a student comes to me, this assessment of proportion is the first step in seeing what I must do to compensate for the limitations that proportion superimposes on the individual singers. In other words, by recognizing what the inherent limitations are, I can apply my method to neutralize the effects of this imbalance in order to pull out the maximum possible performance in the safest possible way from any individual.

Chapter 6: The Physical Aspects of Singing

Proper voice development must follow very specific criteria. By that I mean a certain structure, set of standards or sequence of steps we use to build sound properly. Just as a ballet dancer must use certain muscles, movement and thinking for her dance, so a singer must be just as specific in the mechanical production of sound.

Since most people approach singing in a haphazard or incorrect way, many problems result. And while outlining the proper design for the physical mechanics of singing, I would like also to clarify what is by far the most common problem among singers - over-dependence on the vocal cords for sound production.

Initially, any note that is being sung must have its start at the vocal cords. You can consider it like strumming the strings of a guitar. The vocal cord is "strummed" by the voice and the sound begins. Unfortunately, the way most singers continue the sound of that note is to go to the vocal cords and "strum" them again and again and again. This not only limits their power, range and tonal quality, but also could damage their vocal cords, depending of course on how much they work on their voice.

The proper way to use the voice is to lift the sound using the facial muscles in conjunction with the abdominals once the initial "strum" of the note has been made on the vocal cords. So, as the abdominal and facial muscles lift the sound, it is pushed up to, and across, the upper palate and projected outward, delivering the singer's message to their audience.

The diaphragm must act as a support or foundation for the voice, just as a house needs its foundation. Many singers confuse this with relying excessively on it, or "singing from the diaphragm," which is totally false and will result again in excessive use of the vocal cords and poor quality sound production. Once the lower abdomen and upper diaphragm are used in conjunction with the facial muscles, the sound can be lifted properly and projected outward without any strain on the vocal cords. For rock or heavy metal singers, this is especially important, since the demands of their style on the vocal cords are greater than any other.

Another major area is the proper development and use of the abdominal muscles. Most people have poorly developed abdominals (not just singers either), and for singers, this can limit their progress as much as under-developed vocal cords. Exercises such as stomach crunches, using a slant board (doing sit-ups on an inclined surface), or even various types of calisthenics can develop these muscles.

(Although I possess expertise in a wide variety of disciplines, physical fitness is not one of them and it is my suggestion that you consult a certified physical trainer about how to safely and effectively develop your abdominal muscles.) But there's more to it than simply developing the correct muscles. You must know how to use these muscles properly in singing. Just knowing the theory is not enough, either. To use the dancing analogy again, the dancer can exercise until she is in top physical condition, listen to the best coach and read the best books available, but it doesn't mean she will be able to dance. So it is so with the singer. Until singers understand what is required of their physical equipment and have muscles that can anticipate those demands, they must practice putting everything into play. It's like having all the pieces of a puzzle and knowing where they go; you still have to physically put those pieces into place before the picture is complete.

By the way, as a footnote, I personally feel that instruction in breathing in singing is totally unnecessary, since proper breathing will naturally follow proper use of the musculature. So develop these muscles and use them properly, and proper breathing will ensue. I can't stress this point enough. Proper, powerful singing is a complex and abstract procedure at best, but you can make significant gains in your ability if you use your muscles in harmony with each other. In other words, once the musculature can support the demanding activity required and the singer is aware of the professional standards required to use those muscles properly, he or she must incorporate all of this simultaneously by lifting, placing, projecting and delivering the message to their audience.

Chapter 7: The Emotional Elements of Singing

The previous chapter dealt with the physical components of singing. This one will deal with the emotional aspects of a successful performance.

The emotional aspect is really a continuation of the physical sound and has its roots in the actual message that the composer had in mind -- or more accurately, in his heart when the song was first created.

The performer attempts to recreate that message by singing it from his own emotional sources, and in the case of cover tunes, will add a certain amount of his own emotional flavour to it which is both desirable and inevitable.

Occasionally, the artist will superimpose his own emotional interpretation on top of the original message. Take for example Billy Idol's cover of the song "L.A. Woman" by the Doors. Aside from the differences in mixes and instrumentation, it's the drive provided by the much harder emotional edge and feel of Idol's vocal performance that sets the two versions apart.

However, emotional variance is only one piece of the heart of performance. With respect to the message of the performance or whatever the original artist had in mind for the song, a singer must grasp what it is to the point that he can identify with its meaning and literally deliver it as if it were his own personal message for the audience.

Once that launching point is established, the singer must create an emotional bridge between himself and the audience. This bridge can only be truly powerful if there is congruency between what is going on inside the singer emotionally and what he demonstrates outwardly. This requirement to be "true to form", is a risky proposition since it requires complete authenticity, truthfulness and the ability to be open and vulnerable to the audience. The presence or absence of this bridge is what separates a truly moving and powerful performance from just singing a song. Some of the signsyou will notice when the bridge is present are: increased heart rate, tingles up your spine, goose-bumps or even tears in your eyes.

Once the connection has been made, it is maintained through what I call the cycle of rapport. In order to understand this, you must realize that it's not just the singer who is touching the audience. The audience must, through their emotional feedback, touch the singer as well. This is where the whole issue of sincerity comes in. It's not enough just to "put it out there". The singer must ensure that his message has been received and this can only be done by actually interacting with the audience.

A successful performance then, is like a boomerang. You must be willing to share your heart and soul and be vulnerable and open enough to receive what the audience reciprocates. If you've connected with them, what they return could be eye contact, smiles, a look, applause, their attentiveness, or that moment of silence before applause at the end of a performance, which occurs when your bridge is so powerful that it lingers while the audience comes out of their trance to applaud.

Perpetuating this kind of simultaneous interchange, or really merging with your audience during performance, is what is meant by the rapport cycle.

To summarize then, a successful performance occurs when a singer merges with a song to such an extent that the audience merges with his or her performance. On the level of being, the audience is literally engulfed, or becomes lost, in the experience that the singer is generating at that time. Through a true performance, the singer extends an invitation from his heart in such a way that the audience is irresistibly drawn into the event as an actual participant.

Vocal Science - Flight to the Universe

This is Cupid. Alison has obviously been struck by Cupid's arrow!

One last comment on style. Style is a function of the emotional makeup of the singer. In other words, the type of personal feelings present within him dictates the sensitivity available to a singer. This is why you may be able to physically sing certain songs and not be able to merge with them. Ordinarily, singers pick songs which are relevant to situations they've been in, are in or are heading towards, which lends compatibility to their repertoire and emotional makeup.

I would like to remind you that although the physical, emotional and mental components of a good performance are equally important, in terms of the heart of performance, sharing what is in your own heart with the audience is the most important thing.

After all, the old adage still rings true: "It's the singer, not the song."

Chapter 8: The Intellectual Side of Singing

The mental aspects of singing act in many ways as a bridge for the physical and emotional processes, so that a performance which meets professional standards can be achieved.

One analogy illustrates exactly what this mental process is in the context of singing: a computer operator and the hardware and software of the computer. The operator would be analogous to the emotional aspect of singing, since whether you're a singer or a computer-user your heart is still in the same place.

Computer hardware comprises the peripheral devices, such as the monitor, printer, keyboard and the CPU. Your physical components are your stomach, muscles, diaphragm, voice box and facial muscles. The computer's software resides as bits of information stored on either floppy disks or CD ROM's, which you insert into the computer, or on a hard disk inside the computer. The software can be compared to the mental component of singing because of the way the brain stores and uses information.

One way we learn a skill is by successfully repeating it until we cannot only store a representation of how we did it in our memory banks, but retrieve it successfully as well. The brain can scan images at amazing speeds, but if it can't accurately "access the data", it's of no use.

This is why, when beginning students ask me how much they should practice, I tell them, "Not at all". Practicing at the outset, or any other time when they don't know what they're doing, is merely trying to perfect an imperfect approach to singing. I can access all the data in my students externally and coach them until their internal resources are developed enough (a matter of hours) to know what their mental "software" is all about as well as what it is not.

Although we use auditory sensations as well, singing deals primarily with the storage of images in the form of pictures and feeling sensations. The software "map" of that skill will determine the level of proficiency based on how accurately the map reflects what is accepted as professional standards of singing.

This is why singing instruction varies so much. It's due to a lack of fundamental knowledge of what the exact forms and shapes of these visualizations must be to produce the proper outcome vocally for anyone, no matter what their desired style is.

So besides developing your voice, physiology and emotions; the correct mental visualizations using the right images and sensation will pull out your best in terms of your singing potential.

In concrete terms, you have to understand that when your mental "software" is controlling the sound of your voice, it's manipulating something physically tangible. This physical body (sound) is projected outward from you on a very specific trajectory – again just like throwing a ball. Where it goes depends on your mental "aim" and the amount of thrust you have built up using your upper and lower diaphragm. Using your air as the "fuel" for this thrust, you lift and project that sound so that it resonates in the facial area (cavities around the area of your facial muscles) where it gathers inertia and continues on its "flight path" to its intended destination -- presumably your audience. This entire process must happen very fluidly and can only be achieved when the bodily sensations (regulating the air by the diaphragm), and visualizations (the mental picture of where and how you're projecting the sound) are accurately accessed and used.

So once you get your singing emotionally and physically fit, get your "software" together and "think" your sound properly. You'll definitely sound like you're thinking.

Chapter 9: Vocal Impotence? In Need of Vocal Viagra?

In the previous chapter, I talked about the components necessary for giving a complete performance. In this chapter I would like to talk about an equally important issue. Too many people start a career in singing without learning even the most basic technique. The result is initially really bad singing, i.e. no projection, singing out of tune, straining, not hitting notes fully, etc. The long-term effect is always a damaged voice or the loss of vocal production altogether. The presence of these symptoms will lead to what I call vocal impotence.

Vocal Science - Flight to the Universe

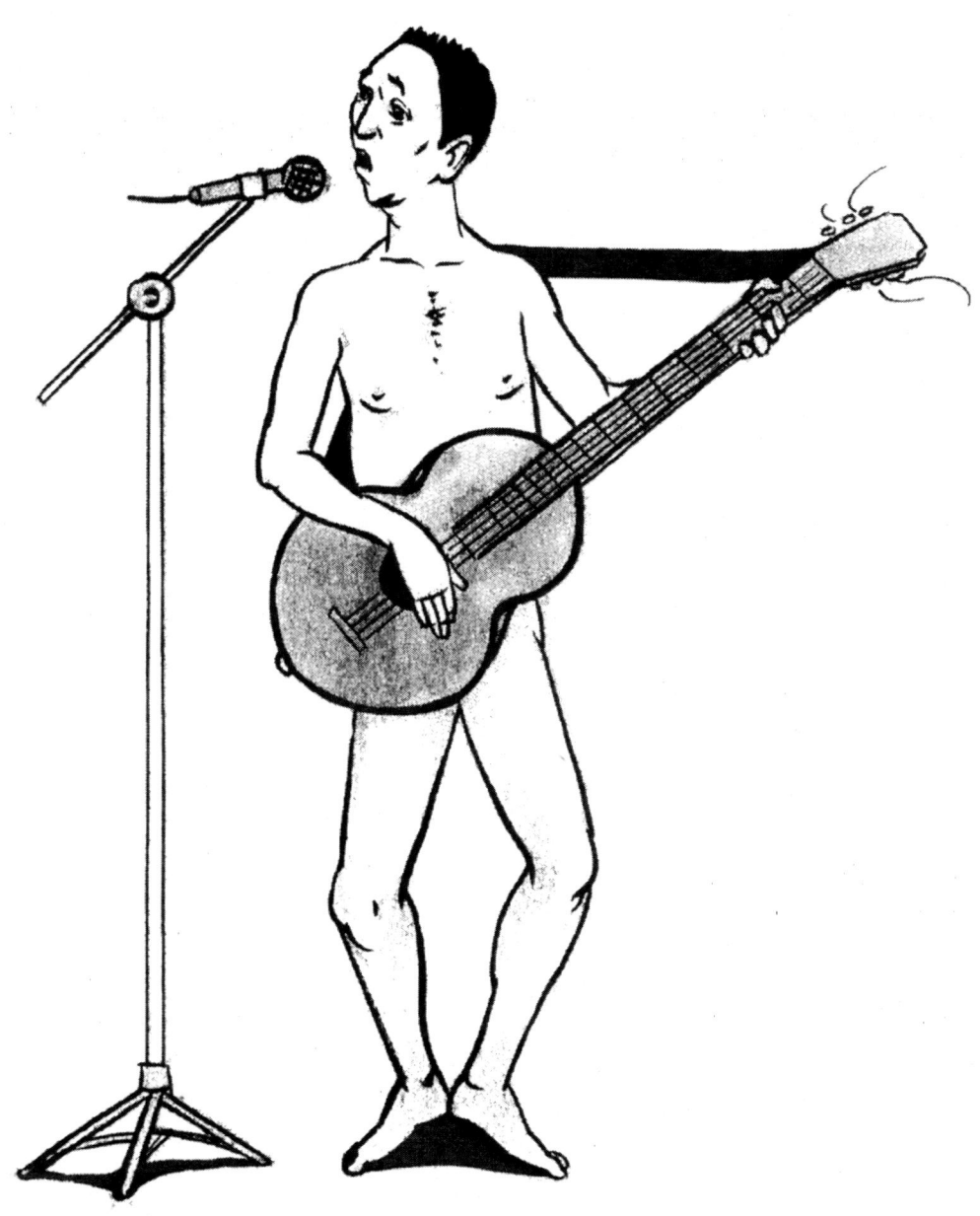

*"This is Chip. He's experiencing Vocal Impotence!
He is trying to hide his affliction with his guitar!"*

It is actually quite simple to explain how people lose their voices. When they sing using incorrect vocal technique, they are putting a lot of strain on their vocal cords, which often results in vocal nodes or nodules. Your vocal cords are like an elastic band - when you stretch them too far or apply a lot of pressure, they usually break or at the very least, will not revert back to their original form. This is what happens when you strain to hit a high note or try sing louder. The vocal cords become curly and weak because they are tired. Usually, rest will work to return them to their original healthy state, but constant abuse will result in severe damage. This is what is happening when you read in the newspaper that your favourite singer is canceling their tour to have node removal surgery.

When someone who has lost their voice comes to me, I offer them a program that consists of three components. First, I recommend some natural herbs, such as Echinacea and Golden Seal Extract, as well as many others, which soothe and repair the damaged area. Secondly, I get them to do special descending pitch exercises that I have developed over the many years of my practice, to release their vocal cords from any pressure. Finally, I teach them correct vocal technique. This ensures that they will not injure their voice again and has the added effect of their becoming a better singer.

It is important that you know why your voice isn't functioning and what you can do to treat it. Many singers have learned incorrect technique or picked up a variety of bad habits over time. Remembering that, contrary to popular belief, dropping your jaw when singing is not good. This traps the sound in the throat and prevents it from being lifted off the larynx to the upper palate. Your voice actually falls between your vocal cords and this will be the beginning of the end of your performance. The resulting sound is, thus, weak and flaccid and incapable of holding the interest of the audience.

My approach to vocal production, which I have likened here to Viagra, is centered on the idea of lifting the sound "upwards" and off the vocal cords and is based on a scientific approach to the physics of sound. Lifting the sound off the vocal cords, through the upper palate and placing it into one of the four main vocal chambers will ensure the longevity of the aimed delivery of the physical sound. This results in a strong and erected sound, opposed to one that is "down", "flat" and, essentially, trapped inside your body.

*"This is Chip after taking Vocal Viagra.
Now the sky is the limit for him!"*

Your diet may also be a reason for your affliction. Mucous buildup contributes greatly to throat problems and dairy products, such as milk, cheese and eggs, will greatly increase the amount of mucous and phlegm on your vocal cords and in your system. Sound can't lift off of thin air; it takes off from your vocal cords. When you eat mucous-producing foods you cannot "lift" each and every note you're singing. This is akin to a ballet dancer trying to dance off a thick carpet instead of a hardwood floor. The best foods for singers to eat are fresh fruits and vegetables, grains, legumes and anything unprocessed.

In my many years of teaching, I have discovered that there are four components that make up the mechanism that allows your voice to reach its fullest capacity: Physical Support of your body, Structure, Placement of the Sound and, as a final outcome, the projection of the sound to its aimed destination. Complying with these components will guarantee that there is no pain or strain on your vocal anatomy. My method of vocal instruction is called Vocal Science (hence, the title of this book), which at its most basic is about bringing out the voice so that it is stronger, longer, fuller and literally erect. When your voice is functioning at its full potential, you will be able sing for hours at a time (without pain or strain) and deliver a performance that will enable you to bring your audience to auditory orgasm.

"This is Cristine. She's bringing her audience to a vocal orgasm. Isn't that the name of the game?"

A Few Words on Herbs

I believe that one of my strengths as a vocal coach is that, besides my musical education, I also have a certificate in iridology and herbology. Thus, my method has become holistic in its nature and the use of natural herbs plays a very essential role in my life and, respectively, the lives of my clients. Over the years, I have learned how to use my invaluable knowledge in herbs to aid my clients with regard to both their vocal performance and their overall health.

The three main herbal products that I recommend to all singers are: Liquid Chlorophyll, Echinacea & Golden Seal Extract and IGS II.

Chlorophyll is the green pigment in plants that harness the sun's energy through the process of photosynthesis. Chlorophyll is to plants what blood is to humans – it performs metabolic functions such as respiration and growth. Interestingly, the chlorophyll molecule is chemically similar to human blood, except that its central atom is magnesium rather than iron. Liquid Chlorophyll oxygenates the whole body and is great for your vocal cords. I use it every day.

Echinacea & Golden Seal is great for the immune system and helps to restore natural moisture to your vocal cords. Echinacea has become one of the best selling herbs in the world. This stems from the fact that

German scientists have demonstrated conclusively the herb's ability to increase the number of white blood cells, which are a vital part of the immune system's defense against invaders. Native Americans considered golden Seal root a natural antibiotic. Through experimentation, I discovered that if you put approximately one teaspoon of this extract on your bare vocal cords (without any water) at least twice a day, it will eliminate dryness and soreness in your throat and vocal cords.

IGS II is a herbal combination (chromium, cobalt, manganese, selenium, silicon and zinc) that I have found strengthens your vocal cords, larynx and, in fact, your entire vocal anatomy.

Needless to say, I often teach students that come with colds and that suffer from allergies. Herbs allow me to heal them to the point where they can actually participate in their lessons and don't have to cancel performances or recording sessions.

A few more herbs that I find useful are as follows:

IMM is great for preventing and fighting colds. It supports the immune system with a combination of vitamins, minerals, herbs and vegetables.

Allergies are especially troublesome because they result in an exhausted immune system, which results in fatigue and low energy, and produces mucous, which coats the vocal cords preventing sound from lifting off of them. I always recommend Lobelia Extract mixed with water for the throat and put two drops in each ear to release stuffed up sinuses. After all, sinuses, i.e. the upper vocal chambers, (cavities), play an essential role in your sound production.

Licorice helps restore the voice, fight flu, colds and all lung problems, as well as helping to balance your adrenal glands, which results in the balancing of your emotions, and also aids your overall endurance. (By licorice, I do not mean the candy you would buy at a corner store, but instead the licorice capsules you would buy from a licensed herbal practitioner.) Many have called this a natural "happy pill" because of this balancing effect.

However, I must stress that you not take any substances without first consulting your doctor and/or a natural practitioner.

Chapter 10 - Vocal Science Magic - Curing the Tone Deaf and Rhythmically Challenged

At the dawn of the new millennium, we can now look back at some of the great achievements of the last thousand years: the microwave; Space travel; the microchip; the Internet; and all of the great medical and scientific discoveries that have extended the human life span and furthered our understanding of the planet on which we live. While we still haven't found a cure for the common cold, I believe I can add two other miraculous discoveries to the preceding list: a cure for tone deafness and treatment for the rhythmically challenged. No longer do those afflicted by tone deafness have to give up their dreams of singing and performing and those who suffer that debilitating condition of a complete lack of rhythm can now finally sing in time with music and even venture out onto the dance floor without any risk of injury to themselves or any innocent bystanders.

The cure to both of these afflictions is, as you have probably guessed, the Vocal Science method. Finally, there is now hope for the hopeless!

But in order to find the cures, we had to first discover the causes. The main cause in both instances is a complete misalignment between the subconscious mind, the conscious mind, the physical body and the voice as an outcome. Kind of like driving a car with wheels that are not correctly aligned. In this case, the car is drifting all over the place and is out of the control of the driver. To solve this problem, one must simply pay a mechanic a nominal fee to put the car on a special computer and to then align the wheels. Human beings are quite a bit more sophisticated than automobiles and require much more special care. As I have said previously, Vocal Science, in a nutshell, is about accessing a cell in the human brain which is located in the speech center, then establishing a connection to the voice, commanding the voice to do exactly what we have programmed the brain to do, then connecting the physical body to the equation and then finally achieving the aimed delivery of the voice.

Over the years, I have created numerous sets of special exercises. The principle of these exercises is the repetition of certain words and vowel combinations in a specific order and specific timing using special body positioning. This establishes a mechanism that is precise and works in a similar manner to a very expensive watch. The repetitional aspect of the exercises is, in a sense, a pre-coding and coding of both the subconscious and conscious memory for the voice and the muscles of the body. This is similar to the way that ballet dancers train using a bar to work on the separate moves and specific muscle groups that will form the basis for all future dances.

This assures that the dancer will not have to consciously think about their next move and will practically be dancing on autopilot and also allows them to concentrate on the character which they are trying to portray. For the singer, it works the same way. If I establish a certain rhythmic pattern within the singer and by constant repetition confirm it on the conscious level to the *total automatic response,* it has been proven to cure any rhythmical problems. Essentially, we have established a precise to the Tee mechanism – equivalent to a priceless Rolex watch.

This is Mickey. Mickey's revealing the magic of the singing alphabet to the world!

To cure tone deafness, I use a similar pattern, but also add some *colours* to my singers' lives. I created a diagram with some circles (each a different colour), which represent musical intervals. (It is especially useful for people that have had no education in musical notation.) This method works more on the subconscious mind than the conscious. After it has been established at the subconscious level, it easily translates itself to the conscious performance. The singer is placed in front of the circles and while I play different intervals on my keyboard, I explain in colours, the combinations I am playing. And again, by constant repetition of the combinations of sounds, durations, and pitches, I confirm the proper picture - now in the perfect tonality in the singer's mind. This stage prepares the singer for the actual singing. Now we have to discover all the possible situations in which these combinations may exist. This will be achieved by singing a range of songs, which encompass all of the above. Afterall, we have only so many pieces of the puzzle to play with! Following this process, the song will be delivered and the SINGER WILL BE BORN!

Chapter 11: The Total Performer – "Get a Life!"

I would like to start this chapter by offering you a seemingly suggestive suggestion on how to become a great singer: GET NAKED! Now before you think that you have mistakenly picked up a copy of the Kama Sutra, please allow me to explain what I mean by this. I am not suggesting that you take off all your clothes and expose your body. (Although this has been a successful tactic for some famous artists.) What I am suggesting is that you must allow yourself to expose your innermost self through your singing. It has been my observation that to make it in the music business and to be a truly moving performer, you must have more than a good voice: you must be willing to create a sense of intimacy with your audience.

I always tell my students that to be a complete performer or, as I like to call it, a total performer, you must have all the pieces of the puzzle. A good voice is one piece. Training and proper care for the voice is another, as are intelligence and image. One of the most important pieces, if not the most important, is having the ability and willingness to share who you are as a person.

Singing is a very intimate activity and that is why many people are often intimidated by the idea of singing in front of other people. I believe it is second only to sex in terms of intimacy. (And a performance is like a polygamous marriage between yourself and everyone in the audience.) You, as a singer, are expressing who you are as a person and putting your emotions, desires, fears and insecurities, on display for an audience. This is not done by all performers, but the truly great ones do and this is what you should strive to achieve at every performance and for every recording.

Some performers are born with this personality trait, this willingness to give themselves to their audience. I actually prefer to have a student in my studio who has this quality over someone who has a naturally great voice but lacks this crucial piece of the puzzle. As I wrote in Chapter 4, I believe that singing is 25% talent and 75% training. For this reason, I can very easily train a person of reasonable intelligence the technical aspects of singing, e.g. tone, pitch, projection, etc., very quickly. It is much harder to teach charisma, personality and openness. But it can be done. Therefore, I actually consider vocal coaching to be only one important part of my job; my work also includes some psychology and counseling. After all, the ultimate goal in this equation is total human development.

Also of importance is that you not only be willing to share who you are as a person, but have something worth sharing. This is why I titled this chapter: The Total Performer: "Get a Life!" You need to have had experiences in your life in order to feed your singing. You need to take chances in your life and experience all that it has to offer. Fall in love! Feel joy! Suffer a broken heart! Explore people, places and things you wouldn't normally dare to experience. Do something out of character for yourself. Witness and try to understand all the positive and negative things about the world. Life experience will nourish your singing (and also help provide material for your songwriting). I always prescribe a diet of lots of water, non-dairy foods and at least 3 helpings of life experience per day to my students. Get out of your rehearsal space because after all, all work and no play makes Jack a very boring singer.

Of course, your performances do not have to be completely autobiographical. An actor does not have to have to feel scared to play a character who is being attacked; instead he fuels his performance with memories of his own anxieties and feelings of desperation. The Total Performer is the performer who is capable of identifying himself with the character he is playing, or lyric he is singing, because he can draw a parallel with experiences he has had in his own life. If you are singing a song about feeling betrayed, you need to be able to identify with the central emotions that are behind the specific lyrics. At the time of your performance you may actually be very happy and in a successful relationship. But unless you have led a very sheltered existence (or a very lucky one), you have probably been hurt by someone whom you trusted. Because you went through this painful experience you can recall how you felt and channel it into a song that you otherwise would have a hard time identifying with presently.

Vocal Science - Flight to the Universe

This is Dr. Zinger and Jack. Dr. Zinger is an expert at prescribing the formula for success!

Life experience can, in some cases, even allow you to transcend the written word and express emotions more complex and affecting than the lyrics you are singing. Two singers performing the same lyric can have a very different effect on the audience. An "I love you" sung by someone who hasn't ever been in love will not have much impact regardless of how well it is sung technically. On the other hand, a singer who has experienced a love similar in nature to the one that Robin Williams' character so beautifully described in the movie *Good Will Hunting,* will be able to re-energize these overused lyrics in a truly moving way. I often feel a shiver down my back when I hear a singer singing a line in a song and it is the sound of their voice and not necessarily the lyrics that is affecting me. You can identify with the emotion very strongly regardless of whether or not it is clearly articulated by an alphabetic language. This is why people can still be touched emotionally by music even when they can't understand the language it is being sung in.

So read the rest of this book. Get as much information from it as you can. Then put the book down and go and get the real life information that is just as vital to being a total performer and a complete human being.

Chapter 12: Born Free - Vocally Yours Within the Structure

Throughout this book I have talked about the importance of correct vocal technique with regards to both performance and the health of your voice. In this chapter, I would like to talk about a problem that I think is a danger to anyone who is taking part in any of the creative arts: an over-emphasis on the technical aspects. Before I continue, I must stress that I am not downplaying the importance of proper technique - it is the basis of any good vocal performance and is absolutely mandatory for anyone who wants to maintain a healthy and fully functioning voice. The world is full of singers who lack the technique to give even a moderately good performance, much less a truly great one. That said, I have also heard (too) many performers that were technically perfect but also sounded stiff, uninspired and boring. As any of my students can attest to, balance is a word that comes up again and again over the course of my instruction. To be a great singer you must find the perfect balance between the technical aspects and the creative aspects of singing.

In addition to my love of music, I am also a huge fan of figure skating and would like to use a personal observation I made while watching the graceful sport to illustrate what I am trying to say here. One evening, I was watching a figure skating competition when the commentator announced that the next skater would be one of my favourite young performers. I am an admirer of her skating and was immediately excited at the prospect of seeing her perform. As I watched her performance I was impressed with her skill, yet at the same time puzzled by what I was seeing. At first I could not understand why I was somewhat disappointed with her performance. After all, she had performed some extremely difficult jumps flawlessly and had definitely not fallen or faltered in any way. As I analyzed more deeply what I had just seen it occurred to me that she was now skating differently than when she had first burst on to the International stage. Her performances had become stiff and over-studied. She was technically perfect, but it appeared that the original spark and energy that her earlier performances had were gone. Where she once "flew", she now appeared to be shackled by all of the technique that her coaches had taught her. I still enjoy watching her skate, but her performances now seem to lack the "magical" quality they used to have. I could almost see the shadows of her coach and choreographer in her every movement.

"This is Terri. She is obeying every rule to the T. Wonder if her coach was an Army Colonel?"

I believe the same problem often exists in vocal instruction: technique is stressed to the point that all creativity and improvisation is wiped out from the vocalist. (This is something that I always make sure doesn't happen with my own students.) This results in stilted performances that are pitch perfect, yet flat sounding, and students that no longer derive any joy or a sense of self-expression from singing. The methodology I employ when teaching my students is a two-stage process that includes what I call structure/structure followed by structure/freedom. When I start teaching a student, I emphasize technique completely. This is essentially an introduction to, and constant reinforcement of, the mechanics of vocal production and is called the structure/structure stage. Once a student has mastered this stage, they are ready to graduate to the next stage, which I call structure/freedom. At this stage, I encourage the student to fully explore their voice and their creativity. The fact that they have mastered the technical side of singing at the structure/structure stage allows them to explore their voice without the risks of damaging it or singing off key, etc. At its most basic, the movement from the structure/structure stage to the structure/freedom stage is the process of moving from being a technically sound singer to a complete performer.

When you were young you were taught your ABC's and learned how to write a grammatically correct sentence, but this most likely did not make you a William Shakespeare or a Margaret Atwood. The same is true when it comes to singing. Proper technique will ensure that you are in tune and that your projection is good, but it will not automatically make you a SINGER in the class of Luciano Pavarotti or Bono. Instead, a basic grounding in good technique will provide you with a launch pad to explore your own individual voice and creative impulses.

When I listen to a singer, I want to hear beautiful singing not perfect technique. I want the singer to have correct technique but I do not want to consciously be aware of it. A singer must have the proper technical elements in place, i.e. support, placement, projection, etc. - but they should be invisible to the audience. Students need to master technique to the point that they can run the technical aspects of singing on automatic pilot, i.e. not have to consciously think about them. Then they can devote their complete mental capacity to more creative elements such as improvisation, nuance and putting real emotion into what they are singing.

A term that I like to use with my students is one that should be familiar to those of you that read music: Rubato. This is a term from Tempo terminology that composers use when they want to denote that a piece of music should be sung in a creative style. It literally means to "rob" the time values by holding back or speeding up at will to colour a phrase – to sing in a flexible, expressive style. I like to tell my students to sing with more "rubato" when I sense that their performances are beginning to sound too overtly technical.

Needless to say, it is important to find a balance in your singing between the technical side and the creative elements. Both are equally important and are essential to becoming a truly great singer. Always make sure to add some rubato to your performances and remember that singing is a creative art form.

Chapter 13: The Total Communicator – Speech to Singing

One thing I have learned in all my years of teaching is that sometimes a student who wants to sing needs to start instruction from a different place than the majority of my students. I can tell from the moment they open their mouth to speak that they actually need speech instruction before singing lessons can even be considered. These people are usually extremely shy and very introverted. They want to sing but can't even communicate clearly when talking.

For these kinds of students, I prefer to teach them how to speak properly first and then once they have that mastered, add melody and rhythm to the mix and teach them how to sing. After all, you have to learn to walk before you can run.

Most people do not even know what it is that is preventing them from singing or speaking effectively. In this case, we would like to familiarize you with some important information about your anatomy, which plays an important part in both your singing and life in general. One of the most important organs is your thyroid, which represents repressed emotions and emotional scars and is located in the middle of the vocal box. The state of your thyroid reflects the state of your being, i.e. mental, physical and emotional balance or lack thereof. When you are very stressed out or experiencing some kind of emotional pain or discomfort, your thyroid tightens and, thereby prevents the sound from an easy movement outward. At this point, the voice literally becomes trapped deep inside.

In these instances, my job as a vocal coach and consultant is not merely to teach proper vocal technique, but is also sometimes to play the role of psychologist. Through counseling, I identify what troubles my client, and then act accordingly. The main thing is to identify what causes some people to get their voice, or true spirit, trapped deep inside their body. Quite often, it is bad memories and emotional scars from their childhood. They may have felt unloved or told not speak loudly or express their emotions. Now they carry their childhood experiences with them in their adult lives.

Culture can also play either a positive or negative role. In fact, it has been my observation that some cultures naturally produce good singers and speakers. For example, many of my best students were of Italian heritage. Italians generally are cultured to speak loudly and express their emotions. It is no coincidence that Italy has a long and celebrated tradition of producing great singers. Conversely, I have found that students from cultures which stress that people should control their emotions and act in a reserved manner often need a lot more work and attention to become even a moderately good singer.

The process of opening up an introverted personality is central to fostering speech development and, later, singing excellence. In situations like this, I begin by again administering the student some herbs such as Kelp, KCX and Licorice capsules, which open their thyroid and balance their adrenal glands, which in turn balances their emotions. These herbs work as a form of "natural Prozac". Secondly, as aforementioned, I very much assume the role of psychologist and aim to discover the root cause of why their voice is trapped. When I have identified the problem, I work at reversing its effects and freeing their personality, spirit and voice.

From a "Frog" to a "Prince"

This is very hard work, but for me it is very fulfilling because it transcends just teaching others how to sing or speak. I have helped people transform themselves into more happy, complete and fulfilled individuals in all facets of their life. I would compare this to the mythical transformation of a "Frog to a Prince". Because the voice reflects the state of the person's being, when you free it, you, in essence, discover the true persona.

Once upon a time, a man from out of town in his mid-thirties came to my studio and asked me to teach him how to sing. Looking at him I found him pretty handsome but not exactly attractive. Everything about his appearance seemed to be in place, but something was missing. During our initial meeting, I discovered what was missing was his spirit. To be more exact, his spirit was hidden behind three walls: his presence, his shell and his being. Therefore, he appeared to be dull, unattractive and boring. Besides that, his voice was hidden in the back of his throat, and, thusly, his speech was very unclear and difficult to understand. During that initial session, after I took the time to make him feel comfortable, he revealed a lot about himself and his personal life.

One of his problems was lack of confidence, especially when it came to the opposite sex. He appeared to be very frustrated while talking about a friend of his, who was, in his opinion, not very good looking, but was very popular with women and had no problems getting a date. My client, who was recently divorced, was obviously experiencing difficulties in this department. So I decided to act upon it. First, I had to identify all the causes of the given matter: introverted personality, hidden emotions, unattractive and slurred speech. Not exactly the qualities that women, or anyone in general, find attractive. He agreed and decided to work along with me.

"This is Al. He's really nervous about asking Megan out. She wouldn't give a Frog like that the time of day!"

The first thing we did was videotape him reading one of my speech scripts, (which by the way, specifically dealt with male and female relations). Not surprisingly, the first take was disastrous. After applying my magic on him, (numerous repetitious exercises, breaking up each and every word into syllables, visualizing each individual syllable traveling up and off his body upon the rules of physics and geometry, and finally explaining the meaning of the actual dialogue), we videotaped him reading the script a second time and the results were stunning! Right in front of me was standing a totally different man, who now looked like a Prince! His posture was different, (he now stood straight), his stomach was tucked in, his head was no longer tilted downwards, and everything about his appearance now projected confidence and strength. His real attractiveness was finally on the surface and if I had not been attached, I probably would have dated him myself! (And broken my own rule of never getting involved with a client.) The frog had instantly become a handsome Prince. From this point, had he continued his sessions, the singing development would have become possible. He went back to home town and, though he promised to come back soon, I have not seen him, although I suspect that he became too busy dating or perhaps even got married by now. Afterall, the sky is now the limit for him!

"10 Hours later and Al is a Prince! He now has Megan eating out of the palm of his hand."

Using Speech Exercises Towards Singing Excellence

I would like to bring to your attention an amazing discovery that I have made through the years of my teaching: it is apparent that human beings communicate in two modes - speaking and singing. Through MY experience, I have discovered that the best way to save and protect the voice and communicate clearly and expressively is to use the Singing Mode when *singing and speaking*. I am not saying you should sing every sentence that comes out of your mouth, but instead use the principles of correct singing, i.e. breath support, structure, placement, projection, intonation, etc., when communicating through speech.

Three groups of clientele come to my school. Some people come to me solely for speech instruction. (Many of whom later decide to take singing lessons as well.) Others come purely for singing in the first place. As pointed out earlier, a third group of students approach me for singing lessons and end up having to take speech lessons before or instead of singing lessons. The common denominator between all three groups is that they will get some speech instruction regardless of whether they are solely studying speech or not and ALL will leave their courses as better, clearer and more communicative people.

During my speech sessions, I use a variety of scripts, which I select after I have defined the needs of the particular student. These scripts are categorized for particular purposes and vary widely in their content.

To give you an example, the following excerpt is from a script that I might use for someone that aspires to go into the broadcasting industry:

"Good Morning. CKIK News Update. Time is 8 O'clock. I'm _____.

Your drive in today is building normally along most routes, with just one minor fender-bender, on the southbound 404 at Major Mackenzie, off to the side..."

This script has been designed to be used by a student with very specific needs. In this case, I would be emphasizing speed (fast breathing), intonation and clarity. This script is actually also useful for singers because of the long sentences. Practice speaking this script will help them to develop their ability to hold their breath for a long time, while singing and will also teach them how to correctly and quickly exchange old air for new to avoid hyperventilation and dizziness, i.e. deprivation of oxygen from the brain, which could be quite dangerous.

The following example may be used for a regular student who is not yet ready to start instruction in singing:

"Oh my. Is there a desk under here? This house doesn't need a maid. It needs a miracle. Or an IBM PS/1 personal computer. Clean-up's no hassle—especially with Lotus Organizer at no extra cost. $179 savings, thank you very much. Sweepstakes to win a PS/1 too. I'll leave them a note. Put it...someplace."

We can then take these short sentences apart and work on each syllable if necessary. A lot of people have problems with their speaking (and singing) because for some reason they do not truly understand *what* they are reading. How can a person interpret a song if they can't truly understand the lyrics they are reading or deliver a speech when they don't understand its meaning! This is often the reason why I have my singing students do speech exercises and read various scripts: besides all the other benefits, it develops their ability to analyze, understand and communicate what they are reading and, later, singing.

The following excerpt is from a script that is ideal for both actors and also people who have trouble expressing their emotions:

"But I'll tell you something, George. No matter what you say about me, I feel so good about myself – better than I felt when I ran from Cleveland and I was frightened to death of New York. Better than I felt when Gus was coming home at two o'clock in the morning just to change his clothes. Better than I felt when I thought there was no one

in the world out there for me, and better than I felt the night before we got married and I thought that I wasn't good enough for you... Well, I am! I'm wonderful! I'm nuts about me! And if you're stupid enough to throw someone sensational like me aside, then you don't deserve as good as you've got!"

Another exercise I use is to get the student to read a script and then turn the page over and improvise its contents in their own words. This builds the intellectual connection between the cell of their brain located in the speech center, their actual voice and their physical body. Putting all these components to work in conjunction and in coordination with each other will ensure a constant and uninterrupted message delivered to its aimed destination. Inevitably, singers will benefit greatly from this exercise as well.

Chapter 14: More Music, More Business

Now I would like to express a couple of my personal opinions and wishes for my clients and present and future associates in the music industry. Having taught in Canada for nearly 20 years, I have more or less become accustomed to Canadian culture, customs and, of course, Canadian music. But what I cannot get accustomed to is the not entirely genuine delivery of art to the Canadian population. Over my years of teaching and being associated with the music industry, it has been a rare occurrence when I have met performers who have been truly talented or, at least, musically educated. Some of the people who have called themselves composers and singers could not make out the difference between two relative notes, let alone sing or play in tune. The ignorance and illiteracy of many so-called musicians was, and still is, a big shock for me. Being brought up and educated in the finest music schools in Leningrad, Russia, I cannot comprehend how these people became artists and have actually sold their "art" for quite a few dollars to a more than willing audience.

Of course, I could simply condemn these "musicians", but they are not doing it entirely by themselves. They are very well supported by the people who are *backing them up*... Now let's take a closer and more in depth look at the mechanism which is the driving force for this global machinery - BUSINESS!

At this point you are probably thinking that I am actually against that 'business' word. I have a pleasant surprise for you: NOT AT ALL!! What I am against is that the word 'business' is not equally supported by the word 'music' in this context. In my opinion, adding the word 'music' right beside the word 'business' in the same font would produce MORE BUSINESS!

Music and Today's Magic Technology

As the years go by, I'm moving closer and closer into the music industry domain and I'm tremendously grateful to those who are in charge of their artists' fine production, and for coming to the realization that the majority of them need work. Perhaps, some of the artists are moderately talented and the majority of them are very good looking, but also quite a few of them have major difficulties when it comes to music and singing! Hard to imagine but in a lot of cases it is true. I have witnessed in my studio people who have been signed or even had their videos playing on MuchMusic who couldn't squeeze out one live note if their life depended on it. How is that possible? Some of them explained that with modern technology, their voices somehow were recorded and obviously enhanced greatly by state-of-the-art equipment. I would like to "applaud" these producers and engineers who have literally been able to perform "miracles".

Now unless we want to produce more Milli Vanilli acts shouldn't we stop right here? They were discredited and had their Grammys taken away on the grounds of fraudulent performance as they were lip-synching over tracks of somebody else's singing. Yes, in a sense, there is a difference as many of today's singers are lip-synching or, in the best case, singing over *their own* magically produced vocal tracks. But what if during their "live" performance the state of the art equipment malfunctions as it did to Milli Vanilli. What will be left on stage? A beautiful and embarrassed "model". In an instance like this, everyone loses - artists, backers, and the audience - and nobody wins, except maybe the late night talk show hosts who will make jokes about it for weeks. However, we cannot deny the fact that some performances, such as fast dance music, do require some lip-synching. It is very hard to synchronize the breath control required for both singing and very active dancing. But if I were a record executive, I would be sleeping more peacefully if I knew that if something went wrong with the backing tracks, my "investment" would still be able to pull off at least a decent performance on their own.

Vocal Science - Flight to the Universe

This is Charlie and Joy. The technology that makes them sound "good" has backfired. Their crew is too preoccupied with how they look to even notice!

How Vocal Science Can Help

At this point, I personally have something very valuable to offer to all of you: **Vocal Science** – the science of the new millennium; a sign of encouragement of more musical education; elimination of ignorance and illiteracy of artist involved in the music industry; a sign of prosperity forward: unlimited success. The Vocal Science method will help artists to succeed in an *accelerated* manner. Working on artists holistically we will be able to induce the maximum power of their physical sound. We will teach them how to get in touch with their emotions while working on their individual style, bringing out the desirable uniqueness of their own. It is no secret that to create a state of the art *artificial* performance is very costly in time and money. Wouldn't it be easier if someone could coach artists and actually teach them how to sing even before the studio time and that nasty upcoming tour which could ruin their vocal anatomy for good, as well as their public image?

We are ready and willing to stand by the artists from the beginning to the end result and guarantee the delivery of the best performance in the shortest possible time. This, in turn, will cut down the cost of studio time, aggravation of those involved and definitely leave more money in everybody's pockets.

Vocal Science - Flight to the Universe

This is Charlie and Joy again. Their crew is amazed that Vocal Science works better than anything technology could offer!

Chapter 15 - Who We Teach

The people that we provide instruction to always fall into one of five groups. Each group has different needs and requires instruction specifically geared to them and based on their specific strengths and weaknesses.

The first group consists of professional musicians. They have already signed with a producer, manager and/or record company and count music as their primary vocation. These are the main clientele and my preferred students. With this group the pleasure is all mine. These students are the reason that I have made music my business. In these situations, I know the exact purpose and aim of the instruction and am provided with the opportunity to explore all my musical abilities, unprecedented skills and education received from the best music schools in the universe. This group is the core of my desire to teach and I hope that down the road they will become my only clientele. My expertise is put to the best use here and I get what can only be classified as joy, by helping these students achieve their artistic and professional goals.

The second group consists of teenagers between the ages of 16 to 20. I call this group the dreamers and I use this term in a positive way because I believe an individual can truly only achieve greatness when they do what they love and follow their heart. (In fact, quite a few students have "graduated" from this group and moved on to the first group.) This is actually the easiest category to teach. They are eager, enthusiastic, hard working and, in most cases, are supported by their parents. In the cases where students do not have the money to pay for lessons, I have always tried to accommodate them in some way rather than deny these "dreamers" the opportunity to pursue their dreams. In order to be able to offer the Vocal Science program to these people, I created my assistants' department. I trained these assistants, who I handpicked from the cream of the crop of my students, because of their musical ability, intelligence and temperament for teaching. They are honest, responsible and deliver my program to the public to the best of their knowledge. I consider them the next best thing to myself in terms of instruction. Because the concept works, they can deliver it competently but not quite to the same high level as its creator would. Of course, I do not expect them to deliver it to my level of excellence. But I will swear on the Bible that the message and concept can still be delivered to a reasonable extent.

The third group is what I call the Young Adult group. They are usually between the ages of 20 and 30 and are usually studying at University or College or are working full-time. These people have generally come to the conclusion that they are not doing what they want to with their lives or are feeling somehow unfulfilled. They may have entered a profession they do not like because it was secure or because of parental pressure. In cases such as these, I feel tremendous pity. They have spent huge amounts of time, energy and money on something they do not want to pursue. They have finally realized that their true desire is music. Even though many are working, they may still live with their parents and, thus, have the resources to act upon their desire and do something that will make them happy and complete. Some actually become professional musicians. Others form semi-pro or indie bands or simply use music to express themselves. With this group, I derive a great amount of joy, for I help them become who they truly are.

The fourth group is the adult group (age 35 to 50). They have established careers and family lives and are not usually striving to make a career for themselves in the music industry. They realize that they are too old to start a new career, but still feel caught in the rut of everyday life, i.e. mortgages, family, long hours, repetitive work. They are looking for an outlet for their emotions and energy. Many are actually having voice problems or have lost their voices due to overuse or work-related stress. They may do a lot of presentations or spend a lot of time on the phone every day.

I have found that the students between 35 and 40 respond best to my teaching because they are still open-minded, want to change, and understand that change cannot come without change. These are the people I often work with holistically, i.e. speech therapy, herbal therapy and vocal instruction in combination. Often, I am able to produce stunning results. I also enjoy this category because these people are from my generation and I find I relate very well to their mentalities, psychology and world views. I am able to help them sustain their professional lives and teach them how to learn to enjoy their jobs. Many often get a promotion or find a better job after my instruction. They are always able to better enjoy music and life in general after taking my course.

Students between the ages of 40 to 50 are often an altogether different category. For this reason, we will call them 4B. They are often bored and tired. Many have children who have grown up and left home and are often depressed and looking for something to do with their lives. Others are physically unhealthy or have a subconscious or conscious feeling that they have not fulfilled their dreams. This group is the most challenging and draining for me as a teacher because they often do not understand the whole process of personal evolution. I cannot say I enjoy this group as much as the others. Of course, I would like to help everybody, but if I had a choice and knew that someone else could help them, I would prefer that. Unfortunately, not too many people have my expertise and knowledge of human psychology in combination with music and voice. I actually used to enjoy this clientele during my

Research and Development stages. But now that I am in my Establishment stage, it is not as desirable as it used to be. Maybe I'm getting older and tired myself? What often makes this group difficult is that they want change without change and are too set in their ways and thinking. Afterall, in many ways Vocal Science is all about a new way of thinking. This makes my job very tiring and draining and, in many cases, they do not appreciate my <u>musical</u> abilities. I often have to be a psychologist, counselor, and even baby sitter before I can get to any music. However, in spite of these obstacles, great success is also achieved with these clients, many of whom have commented that my true calling should be as a psychologist.

The fifth group is the seniors (age 60-80). This group is one that I enjoy for reasons that differ from those of the previous groups. Firstly, they are often simply adorable and beautiful people. There is no pressure because we both know that they are not going to be professionals. They are mostly retired and we can work at a leisurely pace. I admire these people tremendously and love helping them enjoy and enhance their lives in their golden years. I charge them a senior's rate and enjoy every minute of instructing them.

It has always been my moral belief that I should embrace all people instead of just professional musicians and I have made this the mandate of my school. This allows us to contribute to not just the music industry but also, I believe, greater society as a whole. We are glad to accept any student who come to us with pure intentions and willingly and lovingly wants to pick up a new skill and learn to love and appreciate music. Having taught such a wide spectrum of students over the years has helped me become a better teacher and develop the Vocal Science Program to the point that it is actually more than just a singing method.

Epilogue

I'd like to thank everybody for reading this book and I hope it has been beneficial to each of you. I strongly believe that if you drew the right conclusions from everything I've written, this book will change your views on all of the issues concerning your voice and the music business. I wish you all safe and pleasant "flight to the universe", where the sky is the limit.

ISBN 141207001-5